The Time Machine

Text copyright © 1990 by Random House, Inc. Illustrations copyright © 1990 by
John Edens. Cover illustration copyright © 1994 by Tom Newsom. All rights reserved
under International and Pan-American Copyright Conventions. Published in the United
States by Random House Children's Books, a division of Random House, Inc., New York,
and simultaneously in Canada by Random House of Canada Limited, Toronto.

www.steppingstonesbooks.com
www.randomhouse.com/kids

Library of Congress Cataloging-in-Publication Data
Martin, Les.
The time machine / by H. G. Wells ; adapted by Les Martin ; illustrated by John Edens.
    p.   cm.
"A Stepping Stone book."
SUMMARY: A scientist invents a time machine and uses it to travel to the year 802,701
A.D., where he discovers the childlike Eloi and the hideous underground Morlocks.
ISBN 0-679-80371-8 (pbk.) — ISBN 0-679-90371-2 (lib. bdg.)
[1. Time travel—Fiction. 2. Science fiction.] I. Edens, John, ill. II. Wells, H. G.
(Herbert George), 1866–1946. Time machine. III. Title.
PZ7.M36353Ti 2005   [E]—dc22   2005005710

Printed in the United States of America   30 29 28 27 26 25 24 23 22 21

RANDOM HOUSE and colophon are registered trademarks and A STEPPING STONE BOOK and
colophon are trademarks of Random House, Inc.

by H. G. Wells
adapted by Les Martin
illustrated by John Edens

A STEPPING STONE BOOK™
Random House 🏠 New York

Chapter One

Call me the Time Traveler. That is what my friends now call me. But even they do not completely believe my story. Will you? I wonder.

I can only write it all down. I can only hope that readers will see I tell the truth. Readers now or in the future. Only time will tell.

Time. That word brings me to the

start of my story. The start of my journey. The most amazing journey anyone has ever taken.

First, a few words about myself. I am an inventor. A good one. My inventions have won me fame and fortune. But they were nothing compared with my latest, greatest one.

I began work on this new invention two years ago. Two weeks ago I could report success at last.

I invited my four best friends to my house in London. The date was September 15, 1895.

My friends were educated men. A doctor. A writer. A politician. A psychologist. But they listened like schoolchildren as I explained my invention.

"There are three dimensions in our world," I said. "We can see them easily. Length. Height. Thickness. But there is another dimension we cannot see.

"Yet we know it is there. It is part of everything in the world. This other dimension is the Fourth Dimension. It is Time."

I let my words sink in. Then I went on. "We can move through the first three dimensions. We can go backward and forward. We can go right and left. Up and down. Then why can't we move through the Fourth Dimension, too? A train travels on land. A ship on water. A balloon in the air. So why not a machine through time?"

I let my friends think about it. Then I gave them my news. "I want you to be the first to know. I have built just such a machine."

My friends' mouths dropped open. The writer was the first to speak.

"A Time Machine?" he said with a smile. "I never knew you had such a wild imagination. You should try writing fiction. You could create a new kind. Call it science-fiction."

The psychologist chimed in. "I know how you like to joke. Or else I'd tell you to have your head examined. By me, of course. For a fat fee."

The doctor took me more seriously. "You've been working too hard lately. Get out of your workshop for a while. A vacation would do you good. Perhaps a trip."

The politician just said, "Pity there isn't such a machine. I'd like a quick trip to the future. To see how the election next month turns out."

The writer got into the spirit. "I'd like a time trip, too. What a story I could write! Even better, a book. My publishers would love it."

"I'd love to see the medical marvels," the doctor said. His eyes were shining. "Think of it. A world where no one has to be sick."

"Or else a world in ruins," the politician said. He shook his head. "Weapons will be terrible. I wonder if the future holds peace or war? Freedom or slavery?"

"Bravo, my friend," the psychologist said to me. "You've dreamed up a great way to make dinner interesting. Talking about the future brings out all our hopes. And all our fears."

"Tell me, then, did I dream up *this*?" I asked. "Is *this* a dream?"

I took an object the size of a clock from the cabinet. I set it on the table.

My friends examined it. It had a metal frame. Inside the frame was an engine. It was made of rare crystal. A pair of white ivory levers was attached to the engine. In front of them was a tiny chair.

"It's made beautifully," the doctor said.

"Made by hand," I said. "*My* hand."

"But what is it?" the writer asked.

"A better question is, what does it do," I said.

I pressed down on a lever.

At first the frame shook violently. Then the shaking stopped. The whole object became fainter and fainter. It was like a drawing in disappearing ink. Within two minutes it was gone. No trace of it was left.

The writer clapped his hands in loud applause. "I was wrong when I told you to write fiction," he said. "You should be a magician. That trick would make you a fortune on the stage."

"Yes, it is very clever indeed," the psychologist agreed. "How did you do it? With mirrors? And where have you hidden it?"

"Why, it's right where you saw it last," I said. I pointed to the tabletop. "But it is not here in the present. It is here in the future. One thousand years in the future."

"You mean—?" the politician began. Then he stopped and laughed. "You almost had me fooled for a moment. But you would never risk losing such a precious object. Not just to show off for a few friends."

I smiled. "Losing it doesn't matter to me now. It was only a model. A model I no longer need. For I have finished building the real thing."

Chapter Two

My friends gathered around the machine in my workshop. It was exactly like the model I had shown them. Only it was twenty times larger.

"You mean you sit in that chair? Pull that lever? And travel into the future?" the writer asked.

"Or into the past," I said. "Whichever I choose."

"And which would you choose?" the psychologist asked.

"The future first," I said. "It is the unknown that interests me the most."

"And do we get to see it in action?" the politician asked.

"Perhaps take a ride ourselves?" the doctor suggested.

"Not yet," I answered. "I still have a few things to tinker with. Then it will be ready to go."

My friends smiled.

"You still don't believe me," I said. I pretended to be angry. "Very well, then. Come to dinner here a week from now. I promise to show you then that my Time Machine works."

After my friends left, it was my turn to smile. My friends had been right about one thing. I did like jokes.

I had told them I still had to tinker with my machine. But there was one thing I had not told them. The tinkering would take only a few hours. Then my Time Machine would be ready.

Before I started to work, I called in my housekeeper. I told her to cook dinner for my friends next week. The best dinner she could make. And I handed her a note. She was to give it to them when they arrived.

The note said I was sorry not to greet them. But it promised I would join them before the evening ended.

Then I set to work. The work was very delicate. I had to make sure the size of the levers was just right. To the smallest fraction of an inch.

One lever was to start the machine traveling through time. Push it up, and it went into the past. Pull it down, and it went into the future. The other lever was to stop it wherever I wanted.

But I should not say "wherever." Rather, "whenever." Because I would be staying in the same spot. Only the time would be changed.

It was almost four in the morning. I had finished my work. I measured the levers one last time. Now only one thing was left to do. To give the Time Machine its first test.

I sat down in the seat of the Time Machine. I looked at my pocket watch. Nineteen after four. I held my breath as I gripped the lever. I pulled it down a tiny bit.

How can I say what it felt like? Only that it felt like falling. Falling through endless space. My stomach was trying to squeeze into my throat. My mouth was open. It looked like the mouth of a fish. A fish gasping in air.

Quickly I pulled the stop lever. There was a slight bump. The machine stopped.

I looked around me. My heart sank.

My tools were where I had laid them. My coat still hung over a chair.

My workshop was just as I had left it.
My machine was a failure.

Then I saw daylight in the window.
My heart beat faster. I looked at a
clock on the mantle. It said half past
nine. I pulled out my pocket watch.
It read twenty-one minutes after four.

I had traveled more than five hours

in just two minutes. The Time Machine worked!

I suppose I should have stopped then. I should have planned my next move. But I had waited too long for this moment. I could not wait any longer to journey through time.

I pulled down the lever again. This time I pulled it a bit harder. And farther. Time outside the machine speeded up.

I saw my housekeeper whiz into the room. She cleaned it in record time. She shot out the door. It was clear she could not see me.

I pulled the lever farther down. The window grew dark. Then it brightened. Then it darkened again. Days went by like blinking lights.

I pulled down on the lever still more. Daylight and darkness became a blur. The windows and walls of my workshop vanished.

The machine was swaying now. My mind was swaying, too, as if it were drunk. It *was* drunk. Drunk with power. I wanted to pull the lever all the way down. I did.

Around me was a world of wonders. Huge buildings rising taller and taller. Skies changing from dark gray to bright blue. A countryside that grew greener and greener.

What a fantastic show! It was hard to turn my eyes away. But at last I did.

I looked at the dials. They told me how fast and far I was traveling. I was shocked. I had gone much faster and farther than I thought.

I was in the year 802,701 A.D.

Those huge numbers made me lose

my head. I was in a panic. I yanked hard on the stop lever.

I paid the price. The stop was too sharp. The machine tipped over. I was thrown from my seat.

Stunned, I lay on soft green grass. I heard a very loud thunderclap. A shower of hailstones stung my face. It was impossible to see.

"A fine welcome," I muttered. "A man travels over 800,000 years for a visit. And this is the greeting he gets!"

Then the hail thinned. The sun shone through a break in the clouds.

And I got my first good look at the world of the future.

Chapter Three

Through the thinning hail I saw a white shape. Then the hail stopped completely. Blue spread over the sky. And I was staring at a huge white marble statue. On a high base of bronze. A Sphinx. With the head of a woman. A lion's body. And an eagle's outspread wings. It towered above me.

So this was what the future world was like, I thought. The White Sphinx was the work of a great artist. Clearly the future loved beauty.

But then I looked more closely. The bronze base was green with mold. The Sphinx's face was partly worn away.

Had civilization fallen apart? It did not seem so. In the distance I could see giant buildings. They made those of my time seem small and ugly.

I stared hard at those buildings. I saw tiny shapes on a terrace. They were living creatures. People! One was pointing at me.

Suddenly I felt afraid. What would these people think of me? Do to me? To them I was a cave man. Or even an animal. They might want to cage me. Or perhaps even kill me.

I tensed my muscles and pushed my Time Machine upright. I checked it over. Nothing was broken. I could relax. If I found myself in danger, I could escape.

I climbed into the Time Machine and sat down. I gripped the lever. Then I heard someone coming through the bushes nearby. My grip tightened. I was ready for the people of the future!

A man came out of the bushes. I let go of the lever. I could see no danger.

This man was no more than four feet tall. He was very slender. He wore a short purple robe with a thin belt. His legs were bare. Soft sandals were on his feet.

Everything about him was beautiful. But very delicate. Like a perfect flower that would die in a cold wind. But I could feel how warm the air was in this world.

Others came behind him. Their clothes were like his. But the colors all were different. The males and females looked very much alike. I could hardly tell them apart.

There was no fear on their lovely faces. They crowded around me. They were smiling and laughing. I smiled back. How foolish I had been to worry. These people did not know the meaning of fear. They had no reason to hate or to harm.

I let them touch me with their soft hands. I let them touch my machine, too. They seemed to want to make sure we were real. Their voices were gentle and musical. They sounded like birds cooing, as they spoke. Their language was strange to me. I could not understand a word.

Then something began to trouble me.

None of them showed any interest in talking to me. Nobody asked me questions. Nobody tried to find out who I was.

But perhaps they already knew. Yes, that was it! They already had all the answers.

Still, I had to make sure. I pointed to the sun. I wanted to express the idea of time.

My first visitor looked puzzled. Then he clapped his hands in delight. He made the sound of a thunderclap. The others joined in. They made the same sounds.

I was astounded. These people thought I had fallen from the sky. Fallen like the hail. They had the minds of five-year-olds.

I tried to make sense of this. I could not. Then the little people made eating motions with their hands. They patted their stomachs. And I suddenly realized how hungry I was. After all, I had not eaten in 800,000 years! I went with them to their dining hall.

But first I took care to remove the levers from the Time Machine. I put them in my pocket to be safe. Some of these people might play with the machine while I was gone. They were childlike enough to do that.

We walked to the dining hall. Many of the great buildings we passed seemed empty. There were cracks in the windows. The colors of the tiles were faded. I remembered how worn the White Sphinx looked. It seemed that I had been right: This world was going downhill!

When we entered the dining hall, I began to see why.

The hall was huge. It had stained-glass windows and a stainless metal floor. There were panes missing from the windows. The floor was worn by many feet over many years.

The dining tables and chairs were polished stone. Many of the chairs were empty. There was much more food on the tables than we needed.

Only a few hundred people were eating in the great dining hall.

I sat down and began eating. The food was very good. The fruits and vegetables on the table were strange to me. But I found they were delicious. I saw no meat. There were people of my own time who said that eating flesh was wrong. It seemed that their point of view had won out.

There were no plates or knives and forks. Everything was eaten by hand. Cleaning up was easy. Leftovers were thrown into holes in the floor. They disappeared below.

During the meal, I began to learn the language of the future. I pointed to different things. I asked people to say their names. It was slow going. People would come up to me. They would look at me. Then they would drift off. I could only hold their interest for a minute or two.

After eating, the people began singing and dancing. Nobody even glanced at me when I left the hall. I wanted to be alone. I had to put my thoughts together.

There was a full moon out. I strolled along. I saw flowers more beautiful than I had ever seen before. Fruits and vegetables grew wild everywhere. I saw no weeds. No insects. No animals. No trace of any threat to an endless harvest of food.

I thought of the people I had met. They showed no signs of sickness. Or injury. Or even age. They enjoyed perfect health. Perfect happiness. In a perfect world.

This then was the reason for the decay I had seen. The neglect of the buildings. The green mold on the Sphinx's base. People had lost the need to work to make life better. They had everything they wanted. They were happy . . . well, simply to be happy.

Could I blame them? I found it hard to. Yet at the same time I found it sad. This was what humans had become. Creatures of pleasure. They had no thoughts in their minds. Their lives were made up of eating, dancing, singing, playing.

By now I had reached the White Sphinx. I looked up at it and said, "Answer me this riddle, Sphinx. Is this what all of history has led to? All the work of all the scientists? And artists? And thinkers? And builders? Did they do so much to produce so little? Did all their efforts produce a world of people who are forever children?"

I received the only answer a Sphinx ever gives. Silence. I sighed in despair. I would have to take my unanswered question back to my own time.

Then all my thoughts were washed away. A wave of horror hit me. It was like the thunderclap that greeted me when I arrived.

I saw that my Time Machine was gone!

Chapter Four

I could not believe my eyes. Or rather I did not *want* to believe my eyes. The thought was too terrible.

I could not return to my own time. I was trapped in the future forever.

For a moment I froze. I was in shock. Then I forced myself to think. And move.

The Time Machine had to be here.

The people must have hidden it nearby. They were too weak to move it far. Maybe this was their idea of playing hide-and-seek. They were childish enough.

Desperately I searched the bushes around the grass field. Branches scratched my face. Blood ran down my cheek. I hardly noticed. I still had not found my Time Machine.

Sweat soaked my shirt. My eyes burned with anger. The game had gone far enough. I ran back to the dining hall. It was empty.

Where had they gone? I went back out into the night. Another building was nearby. It was a palace fit for a king.

I found the door open. I was not surprised. I had not found a door locked yet. Inside, people were sleeping. There were more than twenty of them. They were lying on cushions on the marble floor.

"Wake up!" I shouted. In my anger I forgot that they did not know my language. "Where is my machine?"

They may not have understood my words. But the anger in my voice was clear. That, and the fist I waved at them.

I made myself even clearer. I pulled one of them to his feet. I shook him hard. Then I let him go. He stood trembling before me.

By now they were all awake. A strange look came over their beautiful faces. I realized that look was new to them. Probably they did not even know what that look was. But I did.

It was fear.

I forgot my anger. I would not be the one who taught these people fear.

I would use a better method to find my Time Machine. I would learn their ways, their language. Then I could tell them how much I wanted the machine. Once they knew, they would give it back.

Besides, I told myself, I was in no hurry. I had traveled so far to find out what the future held. I could take a few days to find out more. I did not even have to worry about the dinner with my friends. I could come home a week after I had left. I was no longer a slave of Time. I was its master.

I patted the shaking man before me on the shoulder. It is the way one calms any scared creature. It worked. He smiled and yawned. Then he lay down to go back to sleep.

Then I lay down and went to sleep myself. Maybe in the morning my Time Machine would be back. Maybe the theft would turn out to be a bad dream.

It did not. But the next day it seemed less of a nightmare.

When I awoke, I went back to the White Sphinx. I was hunting for clues. A group of people followed me. They had already forgotten the fear I had caused. I was once again an object of fun. Like a new toy or game.

I reached the spot where my Time Machine had been. There I saw what I had not seen in my panic. In the soft grass were two tracks. They marked where my Time Machine had been dragged away. The tracks led straight to the bronze base of the White Sphinx.

I banged with my fist on the base. It was hollow.

Now I knew where my Time Machine was. I looked more closely at the base. I saw almost invisible lines. They marked a sliding door. All I had to do was open that door. My Time Machine would be waiting.

But how to do it? There were no handles, knobs, or levers. I had to figure out how the door worked. Or else find tools to force it open.

I turned to ask for help. But the people who had followed me were gone. Then I saw one of them. He was watching me from the bushes. Before he could get away, I grabbed him. I dragged him to the bronze base. I tried to make him understand what I wanted. I shoved his face close to the secret door.

The look on his face stopped me. He looked sick. It was as if I were forcing something horrible down his throat. His eyes begged me to let him go. And I did. He ran away as fast as his legs would go.

I watched him leave. These children would not be any help. Then I looked around for something, anything, I could use. I picked up a rock and banged on the door. It made a few dents. But that was all.

I would have to go back to my first plan. I would learn to talk to these people. I'd ask them to give back my Time Machine. Or else tell me how to get at it.

I gave the door one last bang. Then I tossed my rock away. It was useless.

Then I heard it. Or at least I thought I heard it.

A sound from behind the door. A sound like a chuckle.

It stopped. I pressed my ear against the bronze. But I heard nothing more.

I shrugged. Perhaps the sound had not come from behind the door. It could have been leaves on the trees. It did not matter. I could not worry about odd noises. I had more important things to do.

I soon had another worry on my hands. A much more serious one.

The people who had been so friendly before now stayed away from me. I could guess why. It had to do with my trying to open the bronze door. I must have broken some kind of rule. I had somehow become unclean.

They shrank from me when I tried to make contact. My concern grew. How could I get them to give me what I needed so badly? The knowledge. And the tools.

Then an accident gave me what I needed most of all.

A friend.

Chapter Five

I was walking in the bright morning sunlight. I saw that the weather in England had changed for the better. It was delightfully warm out. All around me people were enjoying themselves. They were playing tag and other simple games. They were dancing to songs that others sang. They were walking hand in hand.

It was a scene of perfect peace and happiness. But suddenly it was shattered by a scream.

The scream came from the river. A swimmer was crying for help.

Amazingly, no one seemed to come. The people around me kept on smiling, laughing, singing, chattering. No one made a move to go to the rescue.

I had to act fast. The river current was carrying the swimmer away. I stripped off my clothes and dove in. I reached the swimmer just in time.

I saw the swimmer was a woman. I carried her to the shore. She was small and beautiful, like all her people. I lay her down on the grass. I rubbed her chilled arms and legs with my shirt. At last she stopped shivering.

That was how I met Weena. She

taught me her name. Then she taught me her language. And she taught me something even more important. That people still knew how to be grateful.

I did not expect to see her again after she went off. These people could not keep their minds on anything. She would quickly forget how I saved her.

But that afternoon Weena joined me again. Smiling, she handed me a wreath of lovely flowers. Then she kissed my hands. After that, she refused to leave my side. She went everywhere I did.

I say this, even though she did not like certain places. She did not mind exploring all the great buildings that I found.

But I also found many round holes in the ground. They looked like large wells. When I looked down one, I felt

Weena's hand on my sleeve. She was trying to pull me away.

I gently shook off her weak grip. I could see only blackness in the hole. But I did feel a breath of air. I took a box of matches from my pocket. I lit one and held it over the hole. The flame was sucked downward. Air was flowing down the hole to somewhere below. But why? Who was there to breathe it?

I turned to ask Weena. She was staring at my lit match. When it went out, her face fell. I lit another and she clapped her hands in delight. Another surprise of the future. These people knew nothing of fire.

But did they know what was down below?

I looked at Weena and then pointed down the hole.

She grabbed my arm to stop me. But I was much stronger than she. I kept pointing. I demanded she answer my question.

She gave in. "Morlocks," she said.

I pointed at her. "Morlocks?"

She looked at me as if I were out of my mind. Then she pointed to herself and proudly said, "Eloi."

What she said gave me an idea. An idea that solved many mysteries of this strange world.

In this world there were two kinds of people. Masters and slaves. The masters lived above. The slaves lived below. That explained why the Eloi did not have to work. Down below, the Morlocks did all the Eloi's work for them. The Morlocks made the clothes the Eloi wore. They made the dishes and cups the Eloi ate and drank from. And everything else the Eloi needed.

I should have guessed it sooner. Even in my own time there were those who saw the world that way. Split between the rich and the poor. Between bosses and workers.

Then another thought hit me. Perhaps the Eloi had not stolen my Time Machine. Perhaps it was the Morlocks.

Yes, that made sense. The Morlocks were the ones who did the work. They were the ones who would be interested in machines.

But what were these Morlocks like? How could I meet them and deal with them?

The answers were waiting for me.

I kept on walking, with Weena at my side. Soon we came upon a huge building in ruins. Its high walls cast shadows as black as night. In those shadows I saw a pale shape. Another man might have said it was a ghost. But I am a man of science. I went to find out.

I stepped into the shadows. Then I realized that Weena had hung back. I turned to look for her. I saw that the Eloi *did* know fear. Weena's face was a mask of terror. Terror of the dark.

I had no such fear. I moved straight into the darkness. I lit a match. And saw my first Morlock.

"It" is what I must call the Morlock. I could not tell if it was male or female. But I could see why the Eloi found it so disgusting.

The Morlock looked like a small white ape. Pale hair grew on its head and ran down its back. Its long arms

hung loose by its sides. Its teeth were
small and pointed. Its huge gray eyes
had a red glow. They looked like they
wanted to pop out of its head.

I saw all this in an instant. Then the Morlock turned and ran from my match. In its panic it ran into the daylight. There it blindly ran into a tree. It shook its head. Then it dashed into the shadow of another wall.

I ran after it. But I could not catch up with it. It disappeared down a hole in the ground.

I was panting. I lit another match and looked down the hole. I saw what I had not seen before. On the side of the hole were small metal handholds and footholds.

This was how the Morlocks could reach the surface. This was how they could return to their underground world. And this was how I could follow them.

If I had the nerve.

Chapter Six

It was hard work climbing down the hole. The metal handholds and footholds were made for Morlocks. And Morlocks were much smaller than I.

I looked up. I saw Weena looking down at me. Her face was filled with horror at what I was doing. Behind her I saw the bright blue sky. It grew dim as I went deeper into the darkness.

Soon I was in total blackness. The humming of machinery grew louder around me as I went down.

My arms and legs were aching. I stopped and lit a match. A little below me I saw a tunnel. It went into the side of the hole.

I reached the tunnel. I ducked my head to enter it. Squeezing through was hard work. The sound of machinery grew louder and louder.

At last I came out of the tunnel. I was in a huge underground room.

I lit another match. I saw giant machines. They were going at full blast. Then I saw something that interested me still more: a metal table with the leftovers of a meal.

The leftovers were bones. Unlike the Eloi, the Morlocks still ate meat.

I bent over the bones. I wanted to

find out what animals they came from. But then I saw the white creatures. Morlocks. Everywhere. Coming out of hiding among the machines. Coming toward me.

I must have scared them at first. But now they were losing their fear. Each time I lit a match they froze. But each time my match went out they crept closer.

They were much smaller than I. I was sure they were much weaker. But there were so many of them. Both those I could see. And all the others I sensed were there.

Now I could tell they were not afraid of me. They were afraid only of my matches. Living in darkness, they could not stand bright light.

But I was afraid of them. Very afraid. Scared to the pit of my stom-

ach. I did not know why. But I felt
there was something evil about the
Morlocks. Very evil.

I wanted to get out of there fast.
But going through the tunnel would

be slow. And slow would be danger-
ous. I had to buy time to escape safely.

I thought of a plan. I let my match
go out. And waited.

In the darkness my heart pounded

louder than the machines. Then I felt their soft little hands grabbing at me.

Instantly I lit a match. Right in the faces of the Morlocks. They were swarming over me like bugs.

They turned and fled. But not before one of them grabbed my box of matches.

I had no time to waste. I went into the tunnel. I squeezed through as fast as I could. I tore my shirt and skinned my elbows. But I made it out the other end.

In the darkness of the hole I groped for the first handhold. I found it. I started upward.

I felt hands clutching at my legs. Pulling me down. I kicked them away.

I dragged myself up out of the hole. Never had daylight looked so beautiful. Beautiful, too, was Weena's joy.

She threw her arms around me.

"I now know why you don't like the dark," I said to her.

But I was wrong.

I did not yet really know. Only later would I learn why Weena feared the dark. Weena and all the Eloi.

But first I found something that made my own fear go away. I found it in a building that used to be a museum.

The building was in ruins. No Eloi was interested in a museum. But whoever built it built it well.

The glass cases were airtight. And none of them were broken. With Weena at my side. I walked among them. I saw the great inventions of the past. Inventions now forgotten by the people of the future.

Then I spotted the most important

forgotten invention of all. A box of matches.

I smashed the glass. I struck one of the matches against the box. The match flared. I breathed a sigh of relief. Weena once again clapped her hands in delight.

As we left the museum the sun was setting. Weena pulled at my arm. She wanted to hurry. She wanted to reach the others before dark.

But it was too late for that. We had wandered too far. Nightfall found us alone in the woods. The rising of the moon was hours away.

Weena clung tightly to my arm. She was afraid of the night. Even more afraid of it than of the shadows.

Soon I knew why. I heard Morlock feet running all around us. And grunting Morlock voices. I felt Weena let go of my arm.

In my hand I carried a metal bar. I had used it to smash the glass case in the museum. But I realized it was useless now. There were too many Morlocks around. Far too many to fight in the dark.

But I did have a weapon that would work. Swiftly I struck a match.

I saw Weena lying at my feet. She had fainted dead away.

And in a circle around us Morlocks were closing in. Wave upon wave of them. Hideous and hungering. I could not hold them off for long. Only for as long as my matches lasted.

I wish I could boast how smart my next move was. But it was very simple. A cave man would have done the same thing millions of years ago.

I built a fire.

I started with dry twigs. Then I added thick branches I snapped off of trees. I soon had a fire burning brightly. Its light protected us from the Morlocks. It was like a fortress wall.

I lay Weena beside the fire. I hoped its warmth would waken her. But it did not. And the warmth did the opposite to me.

I had traveled hundreds of thousands of years through time. I had been exploring the future for days with no letup. I was bone tired. I fell asleep.

I woke to darkness. With so many little hands clutching my arms and legs. And so many little teeth nipping at my skin.

Chapter Seven

I felt for my box of matches. It was gone. The Morlocks were smart. Cunning at least. They had figured out that my matches meant danger. Again they had stolen them from me.

I still had my metal bar. I hit out with it in the dark. I felt it make contact. I heard cries of pain.

But there were too many hands attacking me. Too many teeth. Soon my arm began to tire.

It seemed only a miracle could save me. And something close to a miracle did.

There was a burst of light. And the attacking Morlocks melted away.

For a moment I could not see. I was blinded by the glare. Then I saw that the light came from a nearby bush. The bush had burst into flame.

A spark from my dying fire must have started it burning. The sun in this world of the future was much stronger. The bush was still very dry from the hot day before. Flames leaped up from it. A tree beside it began to burn.

The Morlocks were caught in the wildfire. They were blinded by its light. In their terror they ran into each other. Into trees. Even into the flames.

A few died. The rest found their holes and escaped. I relaxed. The fire

was burning itself out. But dawn was breaking. I was safe.

Then I stopped thinking of myself. I remembered Weena. She was gone.

The Morlocks must have taken her. But why? I knew why they had come after me. They saw me as an enemy. I had invaded their underground home. But why Weena? She would not hurt a fly.

Weena must have known the answer. I remembered her fear of the dark. But it was not the dark she feared. It was the Morlocks.

Then I remembered something else. The bones on the Morlocks' table. Where had they come from in a world without animals?

And I knew the secret of the future. The horrifying secret.

I had been right about one thing.

The human race had been split into two races. The Eloi and the Morlocks. But I had been very wrong about everything else.

Once perhaps the Eloi had been the masters. The Morlocks had been the slaves. But that time was over.

The Eloi must have grown too soft and lazy to feed the Morlocks. And the Morlocks had found their own food. Perhaps out of hunger. Or perhaps out of hate.

The Morlocks still made clothes and other things for the Eloi. But not like slaves working for masters. Instead they were like farmers taking care of livestock. Livestock that they wanted healthy and tender.

That was what the Eloi were. No more than cattle. Cattle kept alive for only one reason. So that in the dark the Morlocks could come for them. So that the Morlocks' dinner plates would always be full.

I smiled sadly. Now I knew why the Eloi had no graveyards. Why there were no old or sick among them. Once I had thought they had conquered death. What a cruel joke. Death, the most terrible kind of death, ruled over them.

In the east I saw the dawn. I shivered. I could not stand to stay in this world any longer. I could not stand seeing the Eloi again. Not now that I knew what they were. And what would happen to them.

Besides, now the Morlocks were after me, too. They would not rest until they got their hands on me. Their teeth into me. Sooner or later I would let down my guard. And they would get what they wanted.

I had to get out. I had to get my hands on the Time Machine.

It was still locked in the base of the White Sphinx. I weighed the metal bar in my hand. Perhaps it could break open the bronze door.

I hoped so. I had no other tools. Unless I found a use for a few matches still in my pocket. They must have slipped out of the box before it was stolen.

The day was hot and bright by the time I reached the White Sphinx. Its worn face seemed to smile down at me.

"Now I know why you're smiling," I said to it. "I know your horrible joke. I know the answer to the riddle of the future."

Then I lifted my bar to smash the

bronze door. But before I could, I heard a sound. A whirring noise. The door slowly slid open.

There was my Time Machine. Right inside the hollow base.

It looked like it was in good shape. In fact, it was in much better shape than I expected. Dents had been smoothed out. Every inch was oiled and polished. The Morlocks took good care of machines.

I let my bar drop. Quickly I checked my pockets. I made sure I still had the two ivory levers. The levers that worked the Time Machine.

Then I stepped inside the base. I had to reach the machine. Even though I guessed what was going to happen. And it did.

The door swiftly slid shut. I was trapped in the dark.

The Morlocks must have been proud of their trap. I heard chuckling grunts as they closed in on me. I smelled their disgusting bodies.

But they were not dealing with a childlike Eloi. I had seen through their trick. I was prepared.

Already I had a match in my hand. When it flared, the Morlocks would retreat. I would be able to put the levers back into the Time Machine. I would give a pull.

And I would be out of this trap. Out of this nightmare future world. I would be heading back to my own world. My own time.

Smiling, I struck the match against the inside of the door.

Nothing happened.

I tried again.

Still nothing.

I had forgotten one detail. One deadly detail.

The matches were the wrong kind. They lit only when struck against the side of their box.

They were useless here. And the Morlocks' hands were already grabbing at me in the dark.

Chapter Eight

I did not try to fight off those hands. There were too many of them. I did not have the time to spare. My only chance was to make my move fast. Before any more of the Morlocks grabbed me.

I felt my way to the seat of the Time Machine. Dragging Morlocks with me, I sat down in it. I found the openings for the levers. I shoved one into place. Then the other.

By now the Morlocks were almost pulling me from my seat. Their hands were cold and damp. Their warm breath stank.

I put all my strength into a sweep of my arm. A savage sweep that sent the Morlocks flying. Then I pulled down on the time-travel lever as hard as I could.

For a moment I thought I would die. The machine was not made to be started that way.

But it worked! That was the important thing. I looked at the dial. The Morlocks were a million years behind me.

True, I had pulled the lever the wrong way. I was going into the future, not the past. But I did not mind. I would take another look at things to come. Then I would head back.

I brought the machine to a stop. I found myself on an empty beach. It was on the edge of a smooth, dead sea. The only signs of life were a few crawling crabs. The sun was a huge red ball. The air was as hot as an oven.

The earth was very close to the sun now. Soon it would burn up. I wiped

sweat from my brow. I was lucky to stop when I did. Before I reached the end of the world. And my own end as well.

I pushed the lever up to send me back through time. Back to the year 1895. Back to the evening of September 22.

This time I watched the dials closely. When I reached 1900, I slowed the machine. I passed into 1895. I slowed it still more. Then I brought it to a sharp stop.

I was back in my laboratory. I got out of the machine. I looked in a mirror. My face was unshaven. My clothes were dusty and torn. No matter. My friends would understand.

I entered the dining room. They were just finishing dinner.

"I hope you enjoyed the meal," I

said. "I told my housekeeper to do her very best."

"It was fine," the writer said. He smacked his lips.

"Delicious," said the politician. He was finishing the last crumbs of his cake.

"You'll have to tell quite a tasty tale to top it." The psychologist was smiling as he spoke.

"I will let you be the judge of that," I said. I sat down at the head of the table. And I told them my story.

When I finished, my friends looked at one another.

The doctor spoke for all of them. "It's a wonderful story," he said. "But do you have proof?"

"I can give you only my word of honor," I said. Their faces fell. Then I added, "Oh, yes, and this."

I pulled from my pocket a handful of flowers. The flowers that Weena gave me after I saved her life. I handed them to the doctor. I knew his hobby was the study of flowers.

He looked at them closely. At last he spoke. "I've never seen flowers like these," he admitted.

"Nor will you. Unless you travel in my Time Machine," I told him. "They are proof of my story."

I looked at the flowers sadly. I thought of Weena. I could almost see her again.

"They are proof of something else, too," I said. "Proof that people of the future still could feel gratitude. They still could feel love."

"Too bad your story has such an unhappy ending," said the writer. He shook his head. "It's a pity about Weena. And even more of a pity about the human race."

"Perhaps I can come up with a different ending," I said. "I'll see what I can do. Please come to dinner next week. I'll have another story for you."

I told them nothing more. Only now will I write down what I plan to do. Then I will get in the Time Machine again.

I will return to 802,701 A.D. I will arrive among the Eloi once more. But this time I will bring them a gift. The gift of knowledge.

I will teach them what earliest man had to learn. I will teach them how to use fire.

Perhaps that will let them drive off the Morlocks. Perhaps that will make them brave. Perhaps they will start to stand on their own feet. Perhaps they will grow to become *human*.

Perhaps.

All I can do is give them the chance. All I can do is put their fate into their own hands.

All I can do as I set out in my Time Machine is hope.

A Final Note

This is not the Time Traveler who is writing now. This is his friend, the writer.

His other friends and I found the story you have just read. It was on the dining-room table when we arrived the next week.

Since then we have been waiting for the Time Traveler. Waiting for him to give us the final chapter.

But the Time Traveler set off on his journey three years ago.
And he has not yet returned.

The End?

Les Martin has adapted *Oliver Twist*, as well as *The Time Machine*, for the Stepping Stones series. Although he has yet to travel through time, Les Martin has visited many foreign countries: Egypt, Turkey, Greece, Russia, England, France—and more! His travels help him re-create the feel of whatever place he writes about. Mr. Martin lives in New York City.

John Edens taught himself to draw and paint as a young boy. Over the years, he has won many prizes for his illustrations. A busy freelance artist, he has always found time for baseball. Mr. Edens lives in upstate New York.